Tiger Dreams

Gerald Rose

CAMBRIDGE
UNIVERSITY PRESS

When I was a small boy living in Hong Kong,

there were still wild and secret places on
the island.

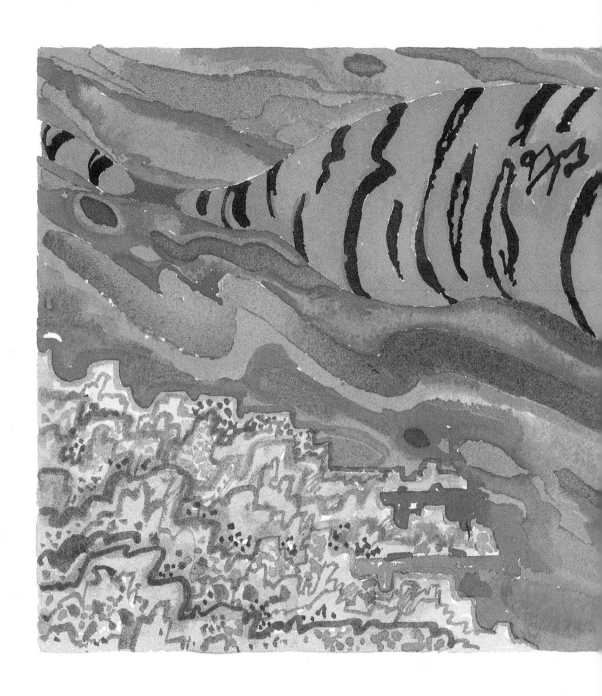

One day, a tiger swam over from
mainland China.

The tiger frightened farmers.

It killed a buffalo.

I was afraid that it might get me.

Everybody talked about the tiger.
We thought that we saw tigers everywhere.

We played tiger games.

I dreamt tiger dreams.

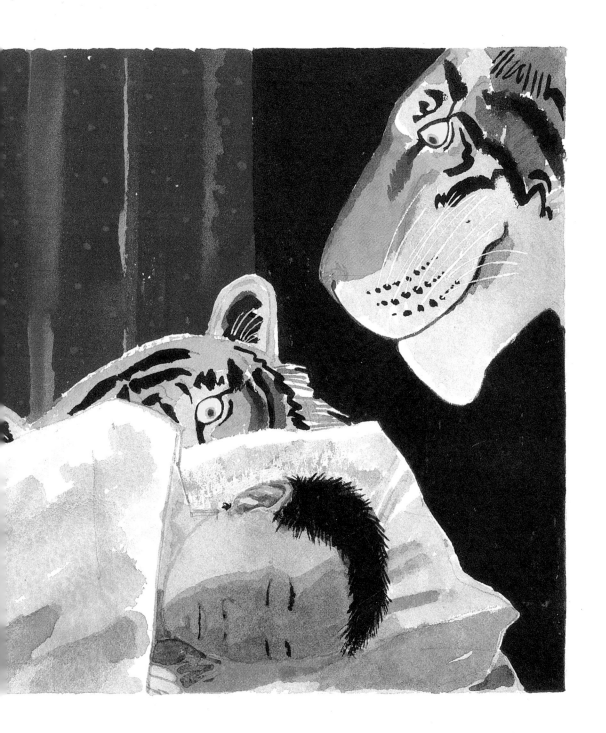

It was very hot.

"We'll sleep on the veranda," said
my mother.

"What about the tiger?" I cried.
"The tiger won't eat you," said my mother.
I was not so sure.

The next day, I found footprints in the mud.

I put my hand into a footprint.
I was getting to know this tiger.

That evening, I saw a tiger swimming across the bay.

I hurried home, looking behind me
as I went.

In the morning, I heard shouting.
"The tiger has been shot."
"They have killed the tiger."

I was sad and felt sorry for the tiger.

I went back to where I had found
the footprints,

but the rain had washed them away.

The tiger that had been so free and wild and beautiful was gone.